Cinder Wellie

Written by
Hilary Robinson

Illustrated by
Robin Edmonds

W
FRANKLIN WATTS
LONDON•SYDNEY

Hilary Robinson

"I love to dance, but more often I go for walks with my Fairy Dogmother, Rocco!"

Robin Edmonds

"I used to live in the city, but now I draw pictures by the sea. I hope you enjoy the book."

Once upon a time there lived a
dairymaid called Cinder.

Her only friend was
Buttercup, her cow.

Cinder was bossed about by
two ugly sisters. "Go and pick the
cabbages!" they ordered.

"Then wash our dresses. We must look beautiful for the barn dance.

Farmer Wellie wants a wife!" they chanted as they danced around.

As Cinder picked cabbages in the
muddy field, Farmer Wellie drove
down the lane in his tractor.

"What a beautiful cabbage picker!
I wonder if she will be at the dance
tonight," he thought.

13

Cinder looked at the clock. Lunch
time! She rushed back to the house.

She was in such a hurry that
her boot got stuck in the mud.

When Farmer Wellie drove past again, he saw the boot. "I'll take this boot to the barn dance, and whoever it fits shall be my wife!" he said.

17

That night, Cinder wept.

"I wish I could go to the dance."

Suddenly, there was a flash! "I am your Fairy Dogmother! Do not be sad. You shall go to the dance!"

21

And with one wave of her wand,
Cinder's rags became a dress ...

... and a cabbage became
her carriage.

At the dance, the ugly sisters tried to
squeeze their feet into the boot.

But it didn't fit. The boot didn't
fit anyone. Farmer Wellie was sad.

Then Farmer Wellie saw Cinder arrive. "That's the cabbage picker I saw!" he smiled.

Cinder tried on the boot.

A perfect fit!

"Marry me!" said Farmer Wellie.

Cinder happily agreed.

And Farmer and Cinder Wellie
lived happily ever after.

Notes for parents and teachers

READING CORNER has been structured to provide maximum support for new readers. The stories may be used by adults for sharing with young children. Primarily, however, the stories are designed for newly independent readers, whether they are reading these books in bed at night, or in the reading corner at school or in the library.

Starting to read alone can be a daunting prospect. READING CORNER helps by providing visual support and repeating words and phrases, while making reading enjoyable. These books will develop confidence in the new reader, and encourage a love of reading that will last a lifetime!

If you are reading this book with a child, here are a few tips:

1. Make reading fun! Choose a time to read when you and the child are relaxed and have time to share the story.

2. Encourage children to reread the story, and to retell the story in their own words, using the illustrations to remind them what has happened.

3. Give praise! Remember that small mistakes need not always be corrected.

READING CORNER covers three grades of early reading ability, with three levels at each grade. Each level has a certain number of words per story, indicated by the number of bars on the spine of the book, to allow you to choose the right book for a young reader:

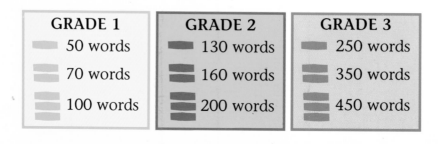

GRADE 1	GRADE 2	GRADE 3
50 words	130 words	250 words
70 words	160 words	350 words
100 words	200 words	450 words